DON'T TAKE MY MAN!

It was eight on a balmy evening. I stood in front of a beautiful walled house at Osu in Accra, Ghana, From the first floor window of the house, a young man, handsome than any other man I had known kept looking at me.

He was my husband. He had been my husband until three months earlier. But now he was having a good time with another girl called Tanga.

Tanga! Would grow to hate that name and that face for as long as I live. Tanga had taken my husband away from me but I was damned if I was going to allow her to continue doing that.

I would fight her for the return of my husband. If Tanga could upset my romantic life like that, what said I could not do likewise?

I would never allow Tanga to take my Jimmy away from me forever, I continued to stand in front of the house and Jimmy kept looking at me through the window of the house. He looked at me as if he did not know me. As if we had never met before. My heart was full of sorrow.

I had heard stories of wrenching romantic disappointments. This was the first time was experiencing it "Why have you done this to me, Jimmy? I kept asking myself "How did it happen? What did she do that I couldn't do?

I Joyce Lamptey met Jimmy Crentsil for the very first time at my sister's wedding He had come alone. I was alone that day too, not because wanted to be alone, but my feelings then made me prefer to be alone.

I was unwell that day, and could not get as actively involved as should have been at my sister Margaret's wedding. Margaret had been looking forward to the day when she would formally belong to her husband, and she had turned out well. Compared to what she had on. I looked like someone who had recently visited a mortuary.

Throughout all the festive activities at the reception, sat all alone sipping an Amstel Malta. I did not see where Jimmy sprung from. All I saw was that he was standing in from of me and looking at me as if he had known me all my life. "Hi" he said pleasantly. "Don't tell me you are okay, because I can tell from your expression that you aren't. Things can't be too bad. Why don't you tell me what is wrong? It could lift some of the burden off your shoulders I was alarmed at the fact that my mood was so easily detectable. "Do I look that bad?" I asked.

Not to people who are not looking at you critically. I was looking at you critically because was happy with what I was seeing. So don't get more alarmed. It might spoil your beauty.

The young handsome man was funny and compassionate too, and that endeared him to me. I smiled thinly and said to him: "If you say so, but I tell you that I am not feeling good. I am just recovering from a nasty bout of malaria "I am sorry to hear that. When I get malaria, you will feel sorry for me. My name is Joyce. Joyce Lampley. Yours is not Mr. Malaria, I hope He laughed softly and sat by me. "How remiss of me. Mine is James Crentsil. Or Jimmy. I can see you are a very interesting lady Joyce. And if you must know, I came to this reception alone "He smiled mischievously.

I pretended not to get the direction he was drifting at. "It is my sister's wedding, and I feel bad that can't help with things the way I would like to, "Oh, is the celebrant your sister "Not just my sister, but we are twins. Jimmy looked at me and then critically at Margaret Meg had removed her veil and was in a hearty conversation with some of her spinster girlfriends. You are right. The resemblance is remarkable. Why did it take me so long to notice that you are twins? Maybe you were not looking at me then," "Damn right wasn't. But I should have. Such beauty as you have cannot lie hidden for long. Even under the scourge of malaria.

I smiled at Jimmy's efforts to flirt with me. "Am I to take it that you are a flatterer of Indies?" "Joyce. Jimmy paused and looked me full in the face. An action that made my heart do double somersaults. "I have never been more sincere in my life than I am now." I looked back at him as he sat there confidently in the chair by me. I realized there and then that I had never met any man as handsome as James Crentsil before. He was tall, athletic and strongly built. His hair was bushy, but nicely shaped. His voice was soothing and his eyes so clear. He looked like a man a woman could lean on in the turbulent waters of life.

What do you think of your sister's wedding The question was so unexpected. "Why do you Margaret and her new husband look a lovely pair? We could look a lovelier pair I gasped. "We? Who are we?" You and me of course. "Are you that much of a despot that you don't give choices?

I am a believer in diplomacy, but not when it has to do with a lady love deeply. I looked at him in utter surprise. "Since which did you love me deeply? "Let's see." he consulted the gold wrist watch. Six minutes, twenty four-twenty five seconds ago."

I laughed uproariously, totally forgetting where 1 was "And Jimmy, you think that is time enough to fall so deeply in love with me as you claim?" "There is a first time for everything. And I will make it happen."

Jimmy got to his feet, grabbed my hands and started dancing with me like the other couples were doing. It looked like this man had forgotten that I was suffering from malaria. But to confess, I felt so joyful in his arms that I would not have stopped him even if I was suffering from the fits:

He left much earlier before the end of the party, because he said he had come to represent a friend of his who could not come. The friend was close to Meg's husband, but had to travel at the last minute. Not wanting to disappoint his friend, he had asked Jimmy to represent him at the wedding Jimmy led me outside after paying his respects to the newly-weds.

He led me to his cur, picked his business card and gave it to me. It showed that he was doing his Masters degree at the University of Ghana in Accountancy That of course explained why a student, young as he was which I believed to be twenty five or thereabouts owned a car. He must have taken time off some lucrative employment to get additional education Holding my right hand in two of his, he pulled me towards him and gave me a light kiss on the check. "I love you Joyce and I hope you will ring me for me to prove it. I want to marry "I know you love me Jimmy, and I think I do too. But I think it is too early to talk about marriage. Besides, Jimmy, with my educational background, I won't be the right wife for you," I stated calmly Why do you say that?"

"I can see what you are from your card I have just completed Senior Secondary School and I should warn you that I was never good at academics. I don't know just how my O' Levels would turn out. But I am not too confident" "I admire your honesty, Joyce. You might not be good at academics, but you may be good at other things. SSCE is enough for me as far as you are concerned." "Don't deceive yourself and me for that matter. Right now that you think you are in love with me, everything about me looks okay to you. But as soon as that love stabilises you will begin to assess me in several ways and see my deficiencies including that of my educational background"

"Well, if that is what you say, then I will help you get the education you want."

With all my dull-headedness?" "I will be the judge of that when the time comes. Let's just wait for your O-Level results. I will sponsor you Thanks Jimmy, but my parents are perfectly capable to cater for my schooling." "Then I will help you tone up your brain, so to speak, if your present stage of education will make you uncomfortable being married to me." With that, he gave me another kiss on the check and drove away.

I was left standing outside there in the dark from where I had watched Jimmy's car drive away. "I love you too, Jimmy." I said into the dark night That night, I could hardly sleep. All my thoughts were about Jimmy

Was it true that an eligible young man like him was single? Didn't he have numerous girlfriends even on the long shot that he was single? Still questioning myself. I finally drifted into a blissful sleep full of dreams about my latest love. I had also made up my mind that I was going to love James Crentsil Later in the morning. I headed for the nearest Communication Centre. I didn't want my parents to hear what I would be discussing with Jimmy. My heart was beating very fast when his phone began to ring Hello I spoke hesitantly into the receiver when Jimmy's voice came over. "Joyce, there is no need for you whisper. I have been expecting your call since" I smiled to myself. "How were you so sure it was me? It could have been anybody else."

"This might not help my ego Joyce, but all the same I will tell you. Since got this mobile phone three weeks ago, you are the third person after my mother and father who has called me on it.

I was not expecting anybody else apart from any of you three any my parents don't call this early." "So what are you doing this early morning thinking about you. What else?" he said smoothly. Too smoothly "Flatterer. He laughed softly "Listen Joyce, I remember one old writer, I guess it was Peter Cheyney. He said a woman will believe anything but the truth. I am inclined to believe him. Women don't like men who tell them the truth."Do you mean you are telling me the truth? "Cross my heart. I paused and chose my words carefully. "Well Jimmy, if it would be any consolation to you, was not able to sleep last night for thinking of you. No man has had this effect you are having on me. I know make myself vulnerable by making this admission to you. But I can hardly help it, I would not like you to disappoint me."

Jimmy was silent for a long while that thought he had not heard what I said. "I dislike being disappointed myself." he said. "I therefore don't do to others what I would not like done to me.

"Thank you then, my Jimmy

"Your what

My Jimmy that was what I said. Are you against me calling you that? I would not like you to call me anything else my Joyce, ho said imitating me. "That is settled then I said I considered all that you said yesterday. Yes, I would like to marry you although it is still a little premature for me to believe it. I will be ready to became your wife if you will give me some time and assistance to pursue a university education too,

"Is that all the conditions you would like me to fulfill? "Yes Jimmy" I replied looking at my watch to see how many minutes had spent speaking on the phone "That condition is okay by me." Then I will have to go now. Bye

No, no wait. Can't we talk for a little bit longer?

I am speaking from a Communication Centre, and didn't take a lot of money when coming down here." lied I lied because I wanted to go back to the house before my parents discovered my absence from the house this early At 21. They would not challenge my going out, but f wanted to keep the James factor a secret till was abundantly sure about his intentions "But why did you not ring from the house, Joyce I laughed to myself. I could not tell Jimmy the reason why I had to come to this Communication Centre I playfully threatened.

"Don't ever question the female instincts if you want to have a successful marriage with me, you hear "Yes. Madam Joyce." Jimmy answered playfully too. "But please hold on a minute, let me say something"

That something had better be good. Now what is it "I will come home to see you this afternoon. Will that be okay with you? "I don't know whether that will be a good idea, you know i…

"Okay that is agreed then. I will be there around two." "Very forceful you are, aren't you?"

"I am not going to allow you to stop both of us from being happy. Now you keep quiet and listen to me say a last thing "You and your last things! You better hurry.

What do you have to say "Just to say I love you" He said it so softly into the phone that I almost did not hear it "Same here too, darling Same here too."

I quickly dropped the phone before my emotions had the better of me Rushed home, carried out my household chores, bathed be coming just that morning but I could not go and eat. Thad prepared a meal of rice and and put on my best clothes. He had said he would come around two in the afternoon, but I was behaving as if he would At a quarter past eleven, I was as hungry as a refugee. Chicken stew, but was waiting for Jimmy so that we could eat it together,

There was nobody in the house at that time. Both of my parents had gone out to thank the many guests who helped to make my sister's wedding the roaring success that it became I was left alone in the house. The reason was that they all thought I had not sufficiently recovered from my malaria. They did not know the part that a new love had played in my rapidly recovery.

I went and sat on the porch waiting for Jimmy. Yet, was worried. There were many things did not know about Jimny except for the fact that he was a post-graduate student at Legon. Even this, I had no clear evidence of except for that compliment card. I also had no idea where he stayed. Neither did I know a thing about his character other than that he was superficially amiable, a smart talker and a gallant gentleman.

Another thing that bugged me was how he would behave if he found out that was the only person in the house. In this age of rape and defilement of women, what would happen if Jimmy got to know that I was alone in the house? Would he behave himself and let our love mature? Why did invite him at all?

All these questions and many more were going on in my mind when all of a sudden saw Jimmy's car behind the gate. My heart was beating very fast and my throat was dry as! ran to open the gate for him. He drove straight into our compound. He was in a blue shirt and dark trousers, with sleek black shoes to match.

His shirt was opened at the front and I was delighted to see that he had a huge and broad chest, covered with a mass of thick black hair. He wore the same watch he had worn the previous day. But around his neck was a gleaming beautiful gold chain, the guy must be rich.

As he got out of the car and walked towards me, I could smell the beautiful sweet scent of his perfume. I rushed into his arm, Jimmy held me tightly in his arms, kissed me on the mouth and lifted me off the ground. I wound my arms round his neck and stared into his eyes. "You look great, Jimmy." I said to him "And you look ravishing yourself, Joyce. I am surprised you say you are unwell." "I was unwell yesterday, but from the time we parted company, have recovered completely. Maybe it's all because of you. I know it sounds foolish, but think you have healed me completely.

"Really?" he asked, and lowered me to the ground. "Do you think I played any part in your recovery?" "Believe me, Jimmy, I spent the best part of last night thinking about you. By one a.m. I was still awake. When! Finally fell asleep, I woke up feeling so well that I am convinced you are part of my recovery He was very happy because of what I had told him. I led him to our sitting room and pointed a seat to him.

"Where's everybody?"

The period I dreaded had come. "Everybody is out except me. They would not allow me to go because they still believe I am not well."

He made no comment to that. I dished the food and we began to eat. Jimmy ate slowly, while scooped mouthfuls For once in well over a month. I realized was hungry. He looked at me in amazement. "Do you eat that much at a single sitting "No sir." I said playfully "But you appear to have revived my appetite"

With a broad smile on his face. Jimmy sat back looking at me. I looked into his face and continued feeding myself The expression in his eyes said that he was absolutely in love with me. With just one movement, be kicked his feet out of his shoes. The next moment, I felt his strong toes playing with mine under the dining table

"Stop being smart." I smiled and tucked my legs under my own chair.

He stood up, and I felt my heart beating. Was he going to show his true colors to me now? Slowly, he came to my side of the table, knelt down beside me and placed his hand on my breast and kissed me fully on the mouth.

I returned the kiss in such a way as not to encourage him to get too excited. When l extricated my mouth from his he looked me full in the face and said: "When are we going to have it Joyce?" felt disappointed. Jimmy was after all as randy as all males.

"Have what!?" I pretended did not know what he was talking about. Have a wedding like your sister's." In fact I felt ashamed for having misjudged his intentions.

Thad my mind on sex, while he had his on a more honourable achievement like a wedding "I thought we settled that this morning. Jimmy"

Oh, did we, of course we did. We agreed to marry after I have also had a university education."

Once more he kissed me on the lips I wasn't trying to go back on my promise, Joyce. I only wanted to test your resolve. It looks like you really want the highest form of education. I will help you to get that."

When the meal was ever, we returned to the sitting room to watch television. We were there when my parents came in. I dutifully introduced Jimmy to them and they seemed very pleased to see him. Jimmy had a lively conversation with my father, who was a retired Education Officer They seemed to have the same views on almost all issues.

I was therefore beside myself with joy when Jimmy finally) had to leave My parents had taken a liking to him as had expected they would, and that filled my heart with joy.

I accompanied Jimmy to his car where he gave me a wad of five thousand cedi notes. When I complained, he let me know that he had a good job with a bank and was doing his university course part time.

When returned to the house after Jimmy had gone, my mother naturally wanted to know more about him. told Mum all I wanted her to know about my new catch.

When I admitted that I had not known him for long. Mum advised me to be careful with him so that I would not get disappointed in future. I thanked her for her love and understanding and showed her the money Jimmy had given to me. She was surprised but did not show much enthusiasm about it.

"Don't make it a habit to be taking that much money from him till you are absolutely sure about his intentions, child Money alone does not make for happiness.

In the days that followed, Jimmy became a regular visitor to our home. Then one day, he invited me to his home.

The young man appeared to have done well for himself. The bank seemed to like his services. His residence was a beautiful walled house at Osu and he lived in it all by himself. Except for a watchman and a garden boy who took care of the place.

1 spent three hours inside the expensively furnished home, but Jimmy didn't make any attempt to take me to bed. We conversed, held hands, kissed but never made love. My respect for him escalated. Before leaving. I prepared a meal and we ate it together in his spacious dining room.

For several months, Jimmy entertained and treated me like a lady. We went to the movies, concert parties, and to the beach. Twice we visited my twin sister and her husband Margaret couldn't say enough in praise of Jimmy. She kept telling me how lucky I was to get such a man.

When I told her that I had not slept with Jimmy yet, and that he had promised to see me through university education first. Margaret laughed "Must he some kind of latter day saint. But if his intentions are genuine, sister, then I should say Ienvy you tremendously," Jimny's father was dead. He had only one half-sister by his mother's present Nigerian bushand. The man had long since gone back to Lagos with Jimmy's mother. That was why I could not meet her yet.

When months later, with the assistance of Jimmy I got admitted to the university to do a diploma course, I was very happy

Times moved quickly.

In my second year, I net and befriended another second year student called Tanga, Tanga Oyetunji. She said she was a Nigerian Tanga was a very good looking girl who was very fair complexioned and hand sharp features at only 20 We became so close that Tanga accompanied me to see Jimmy when I went to visit him at one.

He had by this time finished his course and was now working full time at the bank. When I told Jimmy that Tanga was a Nigerian 100 like his half-sister, he took a very big liking to her Funny as ever. Jimmy made Tanga promise to teach him the Yoruba language, so that he could surprise his sister with it when she returned from Lagos.

Tanga appeared to be very happy with the reception Jimmy gave us too. She chatted happily with him as I went to the kitchen to

prepare something for all of us to eat. I was part host of the house after all.

On our return to campus, Tanga talked ceaselessly about Jimmy Tanga couldn't praise him enough, felt very proud of Jimmy.

But later, her praise of Jimmy became too much that became suspicious of her intentions. You had to watch out for another woman give your man fulsome praise I resolved never to go there again with her.

Two weeks later, after Tanga and I had returned from shopping one weekend she asked if we could go to see Jimmy, I said no, I was beginning to get suspicious of her and to longer wanted her near my future husband. I didn't know what this beautiful Nigerian girl could do to my love. if my back was turned Jimmy in the first place.

Tanga was too beautiful for any sane woman to 1 around her man I even regretted having taken her to see Tanga was not hoppy that we could not go to see Jimmy and left for her hall of residence with the sad excuse that she was tired and wanted to rest And this wits the girl who wanted us to go to Jimmy! She left in such a huff that she forgot her handbag behind.

Curiosity took the better of me and I opened it to see what was inside. I opened the purse I found in it too, and in the purse was a wad of five thousand cedi notes! Crisp new ones like Jimmy had given me when we last visited him! The money did not mean anything I would have dismissed that, but for something else saw in the purse is Jimmy's compliment card!

My heart nearly stopped from shock. At first I thought it was the card Jimmy had given to me, so I opened my own purse to make sure. Mine was in my purse. Neat as ever. I stood there thinking hard. It looked like I was busy closing the barn door after the horse had fled. I stood there nodding. Just then Tanga came back in and reclaimed her bag. Of course I couldn't confront her on the card without admitting that I had been snooping in her bag. But I was sure both money and card had come from Jimmy. Was Tanga having an affair with Jimmy? My own jimmy? Had I made a mistake in taking Tanga to see Jimmy? Obviously Thad. The sneaky thief of a charmer had waited for her chance and visited secretly to work her charms him, I would have to see Jimmy himself as soon as possible to clear this mess up I put a call through to him at the bank, bat was told that he was at a meeting and couldn't talk to me just then, I left a message for him to call at my hall of residence.

The whole day, no call came from Jimmy. That was surprising was he not given my message? That night I could not sleep. Just what was going on? Jimmy sleeping with Tanga because I had not agreed to go to bed with him till I finished my course?

Now, if it was true she was sleeping with him, then where did they meet? When did she get the time to see him? Why hadn't known of this all the while?

They were stupid questions I asked myself really, because if people wanted to be sneaky, they could do it under your very nose and you would not know.

Two days, Jimmy did not ring back. I went to his house on two occasions and was told by the gateman that he had travelled.

Travelled! And he had not bothered to tell me. Had it come to that? Was the game over even it started? Went back to the campus very furious. I did not believe the gateman's story that his master would spend about a week on his trek.

I did not believe the gateman's story because did not believe Jimmy had travelled in the first place. He simply did not want to see me. And I thought I knew the reason why, Tanga

I knew something funny was going on, and if secretly monitored Tanga's movements, she would lead me to wherever Jimmy was holed Tanga meanwhile conducted herself as she normally did with me. On the surface she gave me nothing to suspect her of having stolen my future husband. But of course she didn't know what I had seen in her bag I decided to monitor Tanga.

I did not have to wait long. Two evenings later, when we parted after lectures, she told me she was tired so she wanted to have an early night. I didn't believe her. I was vindicated when an hour later, Tanga, who wanted to have an early night, stepped out at 7 p.m., smartly dressed in a red blouse and tight white jeans. She had great make-up and steel rimmed spectacles on. On her left shoulder a new handbag. She also wore new pair of shoes.

I had no doubt in my mind that Jimmy had bought these for her, I followed her,

Staying a few meters behind her. I watched her intently as she walked out of the campus and headed for the taxi.

She entered a Toyota taxi, and the driver pulled off instantly. It seemed she had pre-arranged everything with the driver. They were off before could get to them. In desperation I rushed to the roadside, chartered a taxi and asked the driver to take a circuitous route to Jimmy's house I was very sure that was where Tanga was going. At the Danquah Circle, I spotted Tanga's taxi. There was no need for any discretion now. It was after all dark I pointed out the tax to the driver and asked him to follow then. I him whatever he charged A quarter of an hour later. I made my taxi stop a little distance from Jimmy's house and got down. could just see Tanga pet down at the gate and the gateman allow her to go in. Tanga disappeared into the house.

From where I stood in the shadows of a big tree, I could see Jimmy standing near the big glass panelled doors of his sitting room. He had his back to me

He was wearing a beautiful green polo shirt. Just then, Tan's face appeared in the room. She had a broad senile on her face because the bright fluorescent fight was on in the room, and I could see her clearly,

She opened her arts wide like a flying cagle-and as soon as she reached where Jimmy was leaning against the glass door, they hugged and engaged in a long passionate kiss. At least that was what I thought they were doing because their faces were so close together. I couldn't help myself no longer. I went to the main gate and started banging on it Jimmy! Jimmy1 cried and banged harder on the locked gate.

"Who be dat" sounded the gruff voice of the gateman "Watchman, it's me Joyce. I replied hoping he would quickly open the gate for me. His expression when he saw me told me I was not welcome "I no tell you say master travel I looked at him sternly. "You can't tell me that."

"But I tell you dat already." he said stubbornly. "You are lying to me Gateman. I saw a lady come in right now, and you allowed her in to see your master. Indeed I can see them in the sitting room now. Yet you tell me he has travelled,

Apparently he was under strict instructions not to let me in "Me I no know wetin you de talk o. Madam, Master no de: Case finish!"

With that he walked back in his cubicle.

I didn't throw any tantrums as I should have normally done. Strangely, I managed to keep a cool head. But I was not going to let things go Tanga's way just like that. I swore. I took a final look at the sitting room window. The couple no longer stood near the window.

I walked back to the main street and called Jimmy from a telephone booth called his mobile phone. The machine was switched on. I wanted the person at the other end to say "hello", for me to be sure it was Jimmy's voice there. He might have been on his guard too. He simply lifted the phone and waited for whoever was ringing to state his or her business. When after about ten seconds I knew that he person at the other end would not speak. I said: "Ei. James Crentsil, is this how the world is? So it is now Tanga…

Click!

Jimmy's mobile phone was switched off. And that was the end of my communication efforts for that day, Grief stricken, I took a taxi back to campus. I went into my room and broke into tears What is the matter with you" asked Selina Pokuna my roommate She has killed me Selina, I tell,

"You look very much alive to me." Selina joked with everything. "Who has killed you? Is Tanga, Tanga Oyetunji my best friend. She has taken my husband Jimmy Crentsil from me." If that is it, then Tanga can't be your best friend." Selina

Selina knew Tanga the same way I did, and was a little surprised that the seemingly decent Nigerian girl could do such a thing "If you don't believe me Selina, go and see if Tanga is on campus.

Selina left me and went out to Tanga's ball of residence to check on her. In less than ten minutes, she returned to confirm that Tanga was indeed not on campus,

Which meant she was still enjoying herself with Jimmy. I wept and wept till my eyes got swollen.

I slept without eating anything that day. The next morning. I resolved that there would be no point calling Jimmy. I would tackle Tanga on campus. I went to the lecture room in the company of Selina. Sitting at her usual comer was the devil, Tanga. She looked so cool, I was amazed at her. Such people could kill and have no thereafter. As the lectures proceeded, I could see Tanga yawning continuously. Jimmy might be yawning at the bank too Hadn't both of them after all kept each other awake with stolen lovemaking.

How I hated that girl who sat there! On several occasions, I exchanged secret but knowing looks with Selina. When the lectures ended. I went near Tanga's desk and said I would like to speak to her. "Go ahead, I am listening," she said without much encouragement. Tanga knew I was wise to her. Ordinarily, she would not have answered me this way if I suggested that would like to talk to her. "No, not here." I said, "Will you come to my hall of residence when we leave here "Is it something urgent, Joyce? You sound worried.

Wouldn't you be worried if you were Uriah and David took your spouse away from you?

Tanga looked at me with a blank expression and said: "I am afraid I don't understand your parable.

I am sure I don't understand myself either," I replied sarcastically. "But you come to my hall of residence all the same and we will both toy to find an answer to what is bothering me. You can help me can't you Tanga? After all you are my best friend."

I will see if will have time around see this evening" "If you don't come at six, then I will come to your hall myself. Provided you would not take another night trip to Osu.

Tanga swung around ina huff "Look, Joyce If you don't have anything reasonable to say, just buzz off will you? I hate these cutting references "Not to worry friend. But please come this evening as you promised, because I have something important to say to you Tanga did not say anything again. She just swung round again and walked out of the lecture hall "Marvellous performance, Selina said as she came to stand by me after tanga left. "I couldn't have done better then that Joyce. But do you think she would come to see you as you requested of her It would be in her own interest to come over. Otherwise, I would make things so unpleasant for her on this campus eh, I would show ber that Royco Shito Mix came to meet Kpakpe shito. Brave Tanga. She came to my hall at six as she had promised. I had not thought she would come. Selina had not thought so either, so she was not in when Tanga came. Tanga was dressed to kill.

Her appearance in my room shocked me so much that I did not know what to say at first.

"Are you going somewhere? Tanga"

"Should that be of any interest to you considering how you behaved to me this morning in class?" "Oh so it has come to this eh? Good friends turned bitter enemies?

"Who started it, if not you Joyce? Was it not your who started accusing me indirectly of things I was not aware of "So would you say you were not at Jimmy's place yesterday night?"

"Have I told you I wasn't?" "So you admit you were, Tanga."

"What if I was?

Her answers were not making me so confident as an interrogator anymore.

But why are you doing this to me Tanga resumed in an apologetic tone. "You know Jimmy and I plan to marry. Yet you meet him secretly without my knowledge after had introduced you to him" At this Tanga laughed. did not understand that laugh then. But then I did not understand this charmer called Tanga Oyetunji.

"Because of you, Jimmy won't see me anymore, Won't even talk to me on the phone"

"I can hardly help it if you have problems with your intended. But don't blame me." "Who should I blame then, Jimmy?

"Not him either

"Why do you say that, Tanga?"

"Let me ask you something Joyce. When we first went to Jimmy do you remember him asking me to teach him the Yoruba language?" That attempt at a cheap he nearly got me to hit that beautiful face which was intent on stealing my husband. "Look Tanga, Tam not an idiot. So don't talk to me as if I am one. How do you sincerely want me to believe that you had gone to teach Jimmy your damned language? Hadn't Jimmy after all made that suggestion in jest "Did he tell you he made it in jest. Joyce?"

"He doesn't have to. And I don't think you went there to teach him any language. If anything you only taught him how to be unfaithful to me."

Tanga laughed again. "I wouldn't teach Jimmy anything he had not already planned on doing. Excuse She stood up

"Where do you think you are going. Tanga? haven't thrashed out this issue yet "I am sorry but I don't have time to waste. I have an appointment to keep."

I thought I knew where Tanga was going this night too, dressed like this. I didn't think she would answer my question. all the same 1 asked again. "Where are you going. Tanga? To my surprise however, she did.

"If it would interest on, I am off to see Jimmy tonight too. We have to tackle chapter two of my damned Yoruba language as you so conveniently describe it I stared at her again I could not move or say anything till I heard my room door bang shut It took me a full hour to decide to go to Jimmy's house again that night. If possible with a policeman to reclaim my man. The time for decency and fair play was long since past.

Surprisingly, Jimmy's gateman let me in this time when he saw me come to the gate. Two Benz cars were parked in the courtyard of jimmy's compound. I did not give a thought to what any of those cars might be doing there simply stalled in towards his front door and started to climb the steps.

Jimmy was the only one in the sitting room when walked in "Hello Darling, long time no see," he hailed me I gave him a wicked look and ignored those provocative words from his lips.

That part of the story was true. But what Jimmy had not told me was that his half-sister Tanga Oyetunji was also a student in my own class, Tanga was Mr. Oyetunji's daughter from a first marriage, and a stepdaughter to Jimmy's mother Things started to fall in place Tanga was a stepsister to Jimmy.

So you see, Jimmy started to speak after wiping off the tears of laughter from his eyes. "Tang becoming your friend on campus was no accident. Her getting you jealous with her praises of me was also deliberate. She wanted you to get spicious of her."

I couldn't believe my ears "So you mean she was reporting everything back to you, Jimmy?

What do you think? Isn't she after all my sister?

It was Tanga's turn to speak now. "Don't think I accidentally left my bag with Jimmy's card in it in your room. I knew what I was doing. From that day, I instructed my brother to start ignoring you, also gave the gateman instructions regarding you.

Oh my God. "whispered to myself "What kind of family would indulge in such expensive jokes? "Our family," Tanga replied happily. The night I left, campus, knew you were following me. Don't you see how I made myself so obvious?

"And to think was playing the IGP by following you secretly. How you might have laughed at me Tanga. Indeed felt sorry for myself. "And why did you think had to stand with my back to the window in my lasted room so that you could see me clearly Jimmy took it up. For one hour, the strange family kept astonishing me.

Hooked at the man as if thought he was out of his senses "Have you been watching some horror movies lately, James Crentsil "Oh, oh, my God. You mean you can't get it? "Can't get what!" screamed in frustration "Just a minute then. He took his mobile phone and made a call as watched him in confusion. A minute later, in came an elderly man. An elderly woman who might have been his wife followed soon after, and of all the people in the world-Tanga!

I looked from the three people to Jimny "Will someone tell me what is going on? Jimmy was by this time sprawled in his chair with laughter. Tanga came and sat by me, while the man who was obviously a Nigerian with such huge tribal marks on his face greeted me

"You must be my famous daughter-in-law, lady, James is told us all about you My mind went back to the cars I had seen in the courtyard when I was coming, it might have brought these people. I looked at Tanga too. She was silently vibrating with laughter. I looked at her critically and locked at the woman, and then at Jimmy.

OH JESUS CHRIST!!!

Tanga spoke "Don't you see, Joyce don't have the need to teach Jimmy Yoruba at all. The rogue knows the language like the back of his hand." She paused

"Can't you get the fact that Jimmy A Crentsil is my brother? And that I have known him years before you ever saw him? It was our plan that we play this trick on you. That was why I laughed this evening in your room at campus, when you said you introduced me to Jiminy.

I opened my mouth in wonder. Yes Timmy had told me his father was dead, and his mother had gone on to marry a Nigerian with whom she was in Lagos.

Tanga, "Look Jimmy, you have to credit me with a little more intelligence than you are presently doing."

"That I do, darling. But what I say you did to offend me was that, you did not believe in my faithfulness to you. Somebody like me who has refrained from going to bed with you till we marry should have had more credibility with you. "Your recent treatment of me in respect to Tanga makes nonsense of that chaste effort."

"You may be right to think that way but.. "Of course I am right!" I answered angrily "Well, if you must know, you are wrong. I did not have the need to learn the Yoruba language at all.

I was shocked. "You are admitting that?"

"Yes, I am admitting that and was happy I made you so jealous. It only meant that you love me very much after all."

"What the devil are you talking about Jimmy.

Jimmy laughed out loud and clapped his hands in glee, as I have known him to do when something amused him beyond reason.

"Can't you get the joke. Darling

"What joke? What joke Jimmy? Look. if you and Tanga think you can pull a fast one over my eyes again, then you are miserably mistaken."

"Oh my God!" Jimmy continued laughing. "I have truly got you there. Now I know what kind of wife I am going to get The perfect one. Most jealous, most faithful. Just what any man would ask for."

I walked purposefully into his bedroom had expected to see it locked. It wasn't I turned the knob and looked in. I did not see who I expected to see I went to the kitchen, the bathroom the toilet and every room in the house. Nobody was there In my disappointment. I went back and plonked myself into the settee opposite of him, I didn't want to sit beside him. Not after he had betrayed me thus.

"Now perhaps, you will tell me the reason for having treated me so despicably these past few days. Mr. Crentsil

"So it's no longer my Jiminy eh

I don't think you deserve that epithet any longer, why not,

"The reasons are private. But I asked you a question which you have not answered."

Jimmy cleared his throat and spoke. "You have done two things in the past week. One of them has offended me and the other has made me greatly happy. I will tell you how you offended me first."

God give me patience to bear infuriating remarks "Look here, Jimmy. What did you say? That I have offended you? Or you offended me? "Yes, you offended me." he said simply

"How?

"If you will only be patient to hear me out. I had only told Tanga to come and teach me the Yoruba language. She told me today that you raised hell over that." I could not stand that kind of insult so I told Jimmy something similar to what had told

If you ever nearly give me such a heart attack like you almost gave me with this lady here, I pointed to Tanga, "I will slice your little head off your shoulders." Right in front of his parents and sister. Jimmy pulled me towards him and kissed me passionately.

When it came to conversation between Jimmy and Tanga, his mother and his stepfather, they all spoke fluent Yoruba. Jimmy was said to have learnt it when he did his first degree at the University of Lagos five years after his mother got married to Mr. Oyetunji, Mr. Oyetunji finally addressed me "We-I mean Joanna my wife and my self-came all the way to Ghana for two reasons. To see the woman Kojo here he pointed to Jimmy-wants to marry, and also to see how he is running this branch of my bank. Your bank, I gasped, when the pieces began to fall into place. No doubt both Jimmy and Tanga looked so rich. So their father was the owner of a bank? A bank which even had a branch in Ghana! Jimmy's mother had indeed married well after the death of his father.

"The Discretion Bank is owned 80% by my family. So now you can understand why we had to make sure that you would be a devoted wife to our son, unfortunately, our own brand of testing our future in laws is a little, what should I say, unconventional. Now that you have been let in on the trick, you will help us to fool Tanga's husband when she gets ready to marry too. You are now part of the Oyetunji family" I couldn't take it all in at once. "So you mean to say you were just testing my faith?" You must understand that your husband is an incredibly rich man who wields great business control. You must be able marry him well to manage the resources. My resources. A sizable amount of which I will bequeath to him. Mr. Oyetunji finished.

"We had to be sure in our own way." Timmy's mother finally said. "Now that you have known us and we have known you, what have you got to say?" I looked at my future family in law and smiled at each of them. But when my eyes fell on Jiminy, I stood up and went and sat on his lap, and warned him.